NIGHT SHEPHERD

A SUNDERED VEIL NOVELLA

Sharon Kae Reamer

Terrae Motus Books/ Overath, Germany

Copyright © 2018 Sharon Kae Reamer

Terrae Motus Books
Oppelner Str. 10
51491 Overath
Germany
https://www.sharonreamer.com

Book Layout © 2016 BookDesignTemplates.com (modified by the author)

Night Shepherd. -- 1st ed.
ISBN 978-3-96575-000-5

"Breton legends speak of Korrigans as doomed human souls, unhappily trapped through tragic death to wander the earth."

~Patricia Monaghan

Part I

Something Lost

FRIDAY NIGHT LATE, at the University of Cologne. The place was dead quiet. Had been for hours.

Something lost, something found, something made and something bound.

The chant ran through my head. I didn't know whose voice was speaking or where it had come from. I shook my head. Too many hours on the bench this week.

The gene sequencer, occupying a square-sized chunk of granite-topped counter, hummed to the end of its program. It made a series of sleek beeps and then went on standby. Sitting next to it, I put the finish to my handwritten notes.

Old-fashioned? Yes. Necessary? Yes. Secure? Somewhat, as long as no one found my combination college-ruled and gridded spiralblock. And even then. They'd have to decode my shorthand. The diagrams might be easier to decipher. Graphic displays are second only to math as a universal language.

I hopped up from my office chair and turned to the standalone deep sink to wash my hands. I took a step backwards when I realized a creature sat on the sink, dangling her legs. She was smallish, not much bigger than my brother Theo's cat Snowy, skin creamy with a pale greenish glow, hair dark with darkish red streaks - or were they purple? They seemed to pulse and change. Disproportionately large feet swung out and back together at the end of those legs. Not large-ish, but large. They were finely boned delicate feet, just much too long for the cat-sized woman-thing on the sink. She stared up at me with her moon-face, not smiling, not frowning, just curious and…wanting. What did she want?

"Hi, uh…where did you come from?"

"You don't know?" she said, in Breton, the ancient language I knew; a Celtic language variant that had borrowings, mostly from French.

I spoke a form of it, passed down from my parents and their parents before them and on back, with a curious family dialect that was a regional mixture from both upper and lower Brittany where my family had roots. The von der Lahns were a curious mixture of Breton-French and German. We'd mostly dropped the really archaic language bits, though. It got too many strange looks from the modern-day Bretons when we tried to speak it.

But the archaic stuff did get a good workout when speaking to Otherworld inhabitants like the one sitting on the lab sink in front of me.

I tilted my head just a fraction and smiled. Answered her in the same tongue. "You didn't come through the Opening. I'd have heard about it."

"Other ways than that," she said. "Wardens don't know everything."

She was referring to us. The von der Lahns had been responsible for rending the veil separating the real world – the waking world – from the Otherworld, which we called Andedubnos, and now we were stuck with the chore of gatekeeping it. This had all happened when my three siblings – my two wombmates and Brevalaer who came later – and I were still in diapers. That didn't mean we had no responsibility. We did. And plenty of it.

And we were old enough now to take our turns as defenders of said Opening, which was to be found in the back of a bar-pub-bistro (or *Kneipe* in German) called *Skogkatt*. Located on our property and just a few kilometers (as the crow flies) from Burg Lahn, our cozy castle near the Rhine, *Skogkatt* belonged to my father and his twin brother and my mother. It didn't get a lot of human traffic because the locals were afraid of it.

I didn't blame them.

At least there was decent food and drink (and sometimes music) to be had while all the defending was going on. We were charged with making sure that the things, non-human and, at best, part-human, that wanted to come through were the kinds of things that we wanted to come through.

"Okay. You came in from a different place. I am interested in that. Intensely. But what do you want?"

Now her look of longing changed to something fierce. Anger and sadness all mixed together. The expression disappeared after an instant. But it scared me. This creature would not have made it through the Opening. Not even close. She wasn't one of the Folk, who we called the *Tud*, which meant the same thing in Breton. Or was she?

She looked similar in size and appearance to one of her fellow creatures, the only one of that kind I'd ever encountered, who made her home in our neck of Ande-dubnos, our private piece of Otherworld real estate that we called the Schattenreich.

We called her Korri. When she'd settled there, no one knew. Ages ago, centuries in waking world time. But Korri had proved useful to the family over the years, so she had been allowed to stay.

So this was another one like Korri. Were they related? I seemed to recall that they were all female, or at least most of them were. Did they all look the same?

"You're a Korrigan," I said, feeling stupid. Of course she was. I was about to ask her name, but that would have been even more stupid. She would probably have told me and then I would have owed her a favor, a *geis*.

She wiggled her toes. "Sticks and stones."

She had several sticks…and leaves…stuck onto the mossy green linen dress, darker in color than her skin, that she wore over a fine, very fine, white wool tunic. No stones that I could see. Standard Korrigan uniform, perhaps.

"Uh…okay. Can we switch to English? Or German?"

The Korrigan nodded once hard. "Okey dokes.

I laughed, despite still being troubled.

"Juliette, Jules, my brave little wolf, omeg —
"

"Hey! Stop raiding my memories. That is so not okey dokes with me"

She grimaced in a facsimile to a smile. "Just wanting a look at your other faces."

I drew a hand over my eyes and took a deep breath. "We're not in a good place to talk. Here. Other humans could see us. It wouldn't be good. They don't know about your kind…or any kind that dwells in —"

"I know that. But no one else here. Can disappear if I have to."

"Really?"

She nodded again in that little-girl defiant way. "You are a Maker."

"A…maker?" The way she said it sounded like a title. Like Baroness or Doctor. I was the first (only by a few minutes) but not yet since my father was still alive and well and would hopefully remain so for many years, and also not yet the second, although I was working on it. Unless I got caught with a Korrigan in one of the Uni Cologne genetics labs. That would probably be considered decent grounds for expulsion.

No telling what they would do with the Korrigan. I had a horrible vision of the tiny creature in front of me pickled in a jar of formalin.

She glanced around the room. The lab was sparkly clean, the black granite counters scrubbed. The glassware was washed, sterilized and drying. A residual odor of butanol had oozed out from under the hood, and the weird burnt curry smell that was also slightly sweet, emanated from my lab coat, my hair, my skin. The smells even tasted sickening. Need a sure-fire diet? Work the bench in a biology lab for a month. Appetite suppression guaranteed. Oh – and your water bill will go way up because you'll stand in the shower for about ten times longer than necessary to get rid of the smells.

To stall for time, I moved next to her. She smelled pleasantly of moss and tree bark and loam. I wondered if she smelled that way in Ande-dubnos. I washed my hands with too warm water and dried them off. I tried to be casual as I plopped into my chair and swiveled to face her again.

"I'm going to call you Korri Ann. Because we call your…fellow, um…," I stopped and waved my hands, "kindred…we call her Korri."

"If you ask, I will tell you my name," she said with a toothy grin.

I laughed. "Do I look that stupid?" I had almost asked, but hadn't quite been that stupid. I'd have to watch out for other mistakes. Other than her being here. Which was a huge mistake. "Are you going to tell me why you are endangering me here in the waking world?"

She held out her hand, palm up. A wisp of gauzy material floated there that looked like a mix of spider silk and Spanish moss. The dirty gray made it look like spun smoke, as delicate as cotton candy. I expected it to melt at any second. The structure unfolded into something that looked like a wing. I gasped at its beauty, a pattern of whorls within whorls that reminded me of a nested triskelion. A shredded area along the inside of the wing, where it would have attached to its owner, was the only flaw that I could see. A single tear escaped Korri Ann's eye.

I stood to get a closer look. The flimsy nature of the wing made me want to hold my breath, but the wing seemed impervious to air, not bending as Korri Ann turned it to and fro for me to examine. A partial memory triggered, but I couldn't call it forth.

"Is it yours?" I asked. I couldn't remember if the Korrigans were winged creatures. I thought not.

She shook her head as more tears escaped. Her sorrow touched me deeply. I suddenly understood what it had taken for her to come here, to risk detection. Other than the occasional sighting in the *Bretagne*, on the west coast of France, the Korrigans were the stuff of legend and comic books – there and only there – and mostly reduced to stories and tales for children. And merchandise for tourists to the increasingly popular area of France caught up in the neo-Celtic revival.

"Okay, Korri Ann. You need to be specific now. I know it's hard for your kind. You don't really live in any kind of linear timeline. Am I right?"

She bit her lip. Then nodded.

"But if you want me to help, you need to stay in the here and now for a few minutes to get this sorted. First —"

"He's gone," she said. "The Last One."

I pinched the bridge of my nose. Doubt that we could get this sorted in a few minutes rose up, making my head buzz like it was full of a swarm of gnats. And so I was well on my way to being truly caught, even without a *geis*. But

I needed to find out what was wrong, before making a commitment to the Korrigan to help her.

I went to the door and peered out through the hall windows. They showed a silent empty courtyard, the tall grasses and landscaped bushes invisible in the darkness. A light burned in a couple of offices in another wing of the building, but that was all. Business as usual, just after midnight. Except for the hired guards, the vigilant knights of the parking lot gates downstairs, I had the place to myself.

Good. But it still wasn't safe. We needed to go someplace else to finish this discussion. I'd have to smuggle the Korrigan out of the building. She'd fit in my backpack, of that I was sure. Whether she'd let herself be subjected to being stuffed in a small dark place and transported by bicycle was another question.

"Are you afraid of being in a small enclosed place?"

Korri Ann's face lit up briefly. "We love small places…where we can hide and watch."

"Wow. Okay. We need to go somewhere else. I can give you something to drink, some sweet tea…"

She seemed oblivious to the offer of drink. "But we need to hurry. You can Make him again?"

"Does he have a name, this 'Last One'?"

"Bugul noz."

"That's his name?"

"It's what he is. *Noz* for night, *Bugul*...I don't know the word in English. Maybe someone who keeps others together and keeps them safe."

"Like a Guardian."

"Like with sheep."

I pinched the bridge of my nose. *Bugul noz.* The night shepherd. I'd come across the reference before, somewhere in Brittany when we'd all been on vacation. One of my brothers' many comic books. The *Bugul noz* had been depicted as an immensely ugly creature, but not evil, and not harmful. I snorted. *Ande-dubnos creatures* and *not harmful* were two phrases that didn't go well together. But how could a creature with such delicate wings be ugly?

Korri Ann tilted her head at me.

"Sorry, just thinking to myself. Is that his wing?"

"No—but same as his material. You need material to Make, right?"

I shook my head to clear it and pushed out a sigh. "We need to go. Can you make yourself smaller, like pixie small?"

Korri Ann snorted in return. "Pixie? I can do anything those hated pixies could do. But one should not speak ill of those who are gone forever." She bowed her head sadly.

I went to the locker and exchanged my lab coat for my fall wool mantle; black and elegant, it had been a gift from Fenris, a thank you for my gift to him of Ickles, the bunny. After stowing the laptop and notebook, I showed Korri Ann the inside of the backpack so she could judge the size. She looked at it with great suspicion.

"Hurry!" For some reason, I was afraid of discovery.

She disappeared the *Bugul noz* wing and then shrunk herself into a bite-sized Korrigan. I gave her a gentle shove with my hand and she hopped into the backpack. No sooner had I closed it, when the door opened and one of the security guards poked his head in the door.

"Are you okay…Frau von der Lahn?"

I breathed out shakily. "I'm fine, thanks. Just on my way home."

"I'll go down with you. Some reports of a stranger in the building – a beggarwoman or some such in weird clothes. And it's not even Karneval yet."

I smiled at his joke and wondered where Korri Ann had gone to first before she'd found me.

After I unlocked my bicycle and rode it out of the parking lot in the direction of my apartment – a miniscule breathing space just off the Cologne Altstadt – the brooding started. Korri Ann stayed put. I hoped she was snug and not too disturbed by my laptop with its metallic parts. I thought I heard her singing weakly.

A shepherd for Korrigans? And he had wings? Was the *Bugul noz* some kind of dragon, maybe? I'd not come across too many dragons in Ande-dubnos. The one I'd recently met had no wings. Not technically a dragon, he was a Naga lord; he'd been pretty buff, too. Then there was Melusine, who we called the Smoke Dragon, although I didn't know exactly why. She guarded the Dreams and hung out mostly in the Between Lands.

Whatever the *Bugul noz* was, he wasn't any more. And Korri Ann wanted me to make him again.

My mouth fell open and the bike's front tire wobbled as I lost control of the handlebars. I steadied them before my bike spilled me onto the sidewalk, and pulled to a stop underneath the *Bahnhof Süd* train overpass. Clothed in darkness and, I hoped, alone, I took deep breaths and wished I hadn't. Sour and unpleasant, the smell of old piss and stale *Pommes* accosted me along with the cold January air. But I swallowed and breathed some more.

I realized what Korri Ann really wanted.

She wanted me to regrow a creature out of myth and legend. A being as old as the land in which it had lived, where the current human inhabitants only had a distorted-through-thousands-of-years memory of what a Path Guardian had been.

Before Christianity had taken the place by storm. A quiet storm mostly, the Breton people were deeply religious. It had been no work at all to convert them. They'd kept their creatures, their mostly invisible spirits, and their Ankous, but it had all gotten jumbled up. Both in Ande-dubnos and the waking world.

Sometimes I felt sorry for all the beings, deities and whatnot that still existed in Ande-dubnos, pitied their existence and how they yearned for the Dreams of humanity to make them more than what they'd become. Waning memories, at best. Degradation to demons, at worst. But my pity was limited to *sometimes*. Mostly I was just happy when they left me alone. Did that mean I hated Ande-dubnos? I'd had bad experiences there lately, and the shock of it all still hadn't ebbed enough for me to be able to judge my true feelings about my relationship to the Otherworld and its inhabitants.

One thing my recent adventures, the terror receded but not gone, had reinforced. Not to go it alone. I needed help with this. Serious help. Who should I call? My siblings? Possibly. But my tiny little apartment was too small for all of us to sit comfortably enough for brainstorming. That meant going to Burg Lahn and risk having my parents find out about Korri Ann. They'd send the little girly-thing back where she came from without a moment's hesitation. And they'd be totally right to.

That left Fenris. He lived a few blocks over from me in a luxurious restored *Jugendstil* apartment. He had a name out of old tales, but Fenris wasn't old. He was two years younger than me, reckoned in waking world time. I still not sure about our relationship, Fenris being my cousin and half human, and that meant trouble. Neither of the parental units had tried to have a Serious Talk with me about Fenris, which I chose to assume meant they weren't worried about the cousin part. The half human part was perhaps a bit more troubling.

Maybe they were waiting to see how things developed between us. Or not develop.

I was, too.

I decided to ping-text him first, and with gloved fingers clumsily stabbed the message into my wrist flimsy.

Are you awake?

Maybe he had company of the female variety. It was Friday night and late.

While I waited for him to answer, a passing train rumbled through overhead and a couple of dubious characters – of the drunken and arrogant male variety – stumbled down the train station stairs. I moved my bike out of the underpass tunnel and into the light. That didn't seem to be a problem for them, as the pair made like an inebriated arrow, wobbly but straight for me. Korri Ann had stopped singing.

My flimsy pinged back at me. I didn't have time for Fenris's reply and readied myself, dropping my bike and backing towards the rough cement of the overpass wall, keeping my eye on the two drunken idiots. I couldn't tell if they were Germans or foreigners in the darkness. It was hard to tell if they were bulky under their puffy jackets. I certainly wasn't man enough to deal with two of them. And right now, nationality didn't matter.

They laughed as they lurched towards me. I dropped into a loose stance, ready to use my one sure-fire karate kick. I did have my best lace-ups on. Random Guy One on my left and Random Guy Two directly in front of me. Who would be first? Just a couple more steps—

Random Guy One screamed and pulled at his hair.

Random Guy Two laughed at his pal and leered at me. His leer got wiped. He screamed and put his hands to his eyes. Blood ran out of his nose.

The other one swayed and shouted in German, calling me a *Hexe* and some other names as well.

But I hadn't done a thing. I still stood there, every muscle tense. My neck ached from the strain.

The two of them continued to curse and moan. Now they were not only drunk but angry. Sweat dripped down my forehead even though my skin felt icy.

I decided to make a break for my bike. I got hold of the handle bars when Random Guy One grabbed my arm.

Random Guy Two shouted. My attacker and I both looked.

A ghostly apparition of a beggarwoman with stringy white hair and glowing red eyes had appeared between me and the bad guys. Her skin was wrinkled, and she sang a very creepy-sounding song in Breton, a Grimm-style gnome if ever there was one. The song sounded like she was counting off the days of the week using a Stockhausen non-melody.

I bit the man's arm and grabbed my bicycle. He and his companion backed off. They shouted *Hexe*! again, and a cloud of fog enveloped them.

They ran, fell, staggered up and ran some more.

I didn't wait around to see if they would change their minds. I sprang onto my bike, riding forward and quickly hung an illegal left at the stoplight. I raced down the narrow street, pedaling as fast as I could go and hoping no one got in my way.

I braked hard at the next stoplight and grabbed my backpack. Loosening the drawstring and peering inside, I breathed out heavily. Korri Ann had drawn herself into a tiny ball. She glowed with the same sort of fog that had enveloped the Random Guys.

A late night dog-walker heading to the nearby park went past me. The piebald Jack Russell terrier lifted its head as if it sensed Korri Ann – which it very well might have – and tried to trot back to us, but its owner jerked on the leash and they went on.

"Are you all right?" I asked.

Korri Ann lifted her head and smiled weakly. I took that as a yes.

"I'm closing up again. We need to go a little further."

I slung the pack on my back again. Awkward to bike that way with my wool coat, I wanted to keep Korri Ann close to me while riding rather than strap the back to my bike rack. My phone chirped angrily from the bottom of the pack. Korri Ann squawked.

I dug around after shunting the Korrigan carefully to the side, and found the archaic digital phone. I kept it because. Reason. I called her Mama. She insisted we all carry one because she hated texting. Still. Papa had adapted without looking back. He'd loved texting, apparently, from day one. Most people, especially people over a certain age, still had phones, but you never saw anyone use them in public. They were considered so outré these days, like smoking but not *quite* as bad.

"Hello?"

"Juliette."

Fenris's gruff worried voice startled me into a gasp. I'd forgotten that I'd texted him.

"Fenris, hey…um, did I wake you?"

"No."

"Oh. Sorry to bother you—"

"What makes you think you're *bothering* me?"

Embarrassment and anger flared. "Well, because it's Friday, the time when people are usually entertaining, sometimes with someone they, you know, are attracted to, and because it's late and—"

"Entertaining?" He laughed. "Is something wrong?"

I pushed down my irritation and told him about the Korrigan, just a rough version about her showing up in the lab, and that I needed help.

"Should I pick you up?" he asked, his gruffness gone.

"I'm on my bike. I can be there in about ten minutes or so."

"Your bike? Did you know winter is officially declared as having started over a month ago?"

"Yeah. I kinda knew that. I'm toasty warm with that lovely coat you gave me."

"Would you like tea or coffee?"

"Stronger stuff."

"Gaelic coffee?"

"Perfect."

Fenris opened the door to his flat as I was coding the bike lock.

"You can bring it in. No one would steal it then."

"If they try to steal it, they'll get a shock, and the alarm on the lock is loud enough to wake the dead and the scare the shit out of the undead."

He snorted. "Your bicycle looks like it survived the last Ice Age. I doubt anyone would even bother to steal that one."

"Not true. In Cologne, they'll steal any bike. Anytime."

My brand new, most expensive bike got stolen over a year ago. The new, less expensive one just a few months after that. Then I bought a cheap city bike from a former student and got my cousin Jeremiah to hack an off-the-shelf lock to make a few enhancements, one of which was the alarm and the mild electric shock. He'd done it no charge since he'd also lost a couple of bicycles to Cologne bike thieves.

I walked up the front steps and Fenris gestured me inside. He was dressed casually, jeans (black) and a cashmere (his weakness) pullover, with a black Tee underneath. So *not* in his pajamas. I laid down the pack on the gleaming black and white tiled foyer floor and began shedding; fleece headband, gloves, my coat. But before I got past the gloves, I was drawn into a tight warm embrace. Warm kisses followed. He had that familiar, wild woods scent of rich earth and fallen leaves. He tasted as good as his arms felt around me. My fingers tingled underneath the fleece gloves I still wore.

"Hey. Fenris," I said when breath returned.

"Juliette." He touched my nose with his forefinger and tugged on the headband. "See?"

"See what?"

"As of now, I am *entertaining*. Someone, you know —

"Thanks. I, uh…" Looking for a way to best describe my mixed feelings without going maudlin, I failed utterly and dripped awkward onto the tiles.

He helped me take off my coat, and hung it on an antique dark wooden coatrack along with my scarf. The coatrack was kind of ugly and so unlike Fenris's refined modern taste that I figured it was probably an heirloom. I'd never asked him about it.

I stuck the gloves and headband in the coat pockets while he waited. I picked up the backpack and pointed to it. "One Korrigan. Many problems."

His look of disgust would have been comical if it didn't have a frightening, wolflike edge to it.

"What?" I asked.

"Why did you bring a Korrigan here?"

"Um. Because? She needs my – our – help?"

He snorted again and turned away, going through a side door that led into his sitting room. It was lit in candlelight from real wall sconces and a few thick square (black, of course) candles on the table by the picture windows facing out to the garden. Nothing to see there in the darkness, but I remembered the recent enchanted moonlit evening when we'd sat here and looked out over a pristine snowfall-laden vista. A small vista since it was a city garden, but it had been magical and intimate.

I followed him in and sat across from him on the facing couch, both couches stylish and comfortable and separated by a shiny black (I'm not using the word lacquer, here, as that sounds cheesy – and nothing about Fenris was cheesy) massive coffee table. It held a tray with two mugs of steaming (and, I assumed) cream and whiskey-laden coffee.

He leaned back, an arm across the back of the couch, his look questioning.

I held up a finger and opened the pack. Korri Ann looked up, her eyes bright with anticipation and fear. I held out my hand, palm up. She shook her head, her arms crossed. What? Was she going to do an old-timey *I Dream of Jeannie* exit? No way. I'd already told her to back off from raiding my memories, and it would have pissed me off particularly if she knew I'd streamed the ancient series hundreds of times. I don't know why. Nothing really to be embarrassed about. Except for that one time in sixth grade I had

Mama buy me a harem-type Karneval outfit that I'd doctored to look exactly like Jeannie's.

No, Korri Ann didn't. She made her way out of the pack using one of the drawstrings as a climbing aid. She looked around quickly, spied Fenris, and then hopped onto the couch. Once there, she returned to being cat-sized, like an image in a pool of water that shimmered and then changed.

She sat next to me and glared at Fenris, her legs dangling over the edge of the couch.

I picked up my black (yes, lacquered) mug and lifted it in a quick toast to Fenris. He didn't move to do the same.

"Would you like something to drink?" he asked Korri Ann, a broad hint of sarcasm in his voice.

He spoke to her in Breton. I'd not been aware he could speak the language, but, yeah, it made sense. He was family, through and through. Except for the non-human part of him.

"*Eigi einhamr*," she said, and nicked her head in a bare show of respect.

"Have you come to steal babies?" Fenris growled.

I took a sip of the still hot coffee and felt the tingle of the alcohol going down, the warm and sweet aroma in stark contrast to the sticky sour atmosphere in the room. The suddenly silent room. I wished for snow and intimacy. And that Korri Ann would go away. Now.

"We don't steal babies," she said and her face heated in anger. "Only take those offered. Why do your kind abandon babies?"

Fenris sat straighter, his eyes wary. He'd been challenged. And I could see doubt in his eyes. "If you speak truth, then..."

She nodded. "We do not deceive in that way, as you must know. Only in self-defense, may we speak untruth. But there are no more babies to be abandoned in these times. Not in the Lands Beyond."

He nodded in acknowledgement of the fertility problems with those of his Folk in the Lands Beyond, the *Jötnar*, or so-called Frost Giants. They were neither frosty nor particular giant-sized, so I had no idea where the name had come from. Maybe the Germanic tribes and Norse tribes had meant something else, or it was a translation problem. Or Jacob Grimm and his colleagues just got it wrong.

The Korrigans had often been accused of stealing human babies, but Korri – *our* Schattenreich Korrigan – had told me once that human babies did not interest them enough to *steal* them. And had sniffed loudly at the thought. I believed her, especially since baby-stealing was not a deed attributed only to beings like the Korrigans. Trolls, demons, gnomes, fairies, etc. had all been accused in times past.

My father concurred with some folklorists who claimed that the stolen babies (substituted with changelings) meme was a coordinated – and mostly successful – anti-propaganda campaign by medieval clergy to encourage the peasantry to have their children baptized. It could also have been an older propaganda campaign, as in pre-Christian older, to explain away defective babies (and justify abandoning them).

But I doubted that the Korrigans had anything to do with baby-stealing in the waking world. Adult males – they were fair prey – were another story. I gave Fenris a brief but thrilling account of Korri Ann's help against my attackers.

Fenris glared at me, but the effect was ruined by the worry in his eyes. We'd had this discussion before. I insisted on working late. He insisted that he'd come pick me up in his chauffeured (black) Audi sedan. Since neither chauffeur nor sedan lived in the flat with him,

I assumed they were housed elsewhere, but not too far away. We'd not been able to come to a satisfying *compromise* on the subject yet. But it wasn't for lack of trying. The arguments usually ended up being defused by kisses. No complaining about that. Nope.

"And now you owe her for her help?" he asked.

I shrugged. "Not directly. But I'd already decided to help her. Only problem is, I'm not sure I can."

"Make *Bugul noz*," Korri Ann said and the tears welled up again. "Gone. Gone forever."

I prompted her to show Fenris the wing.

He lifted an eyebrow after he saw it. "Can't say I ever saw…is it a him?"

She nodded.

"Only those comic book creatures," he said. "Supposed to be ugly."

Korri Ann stiffened and shook her little fists. "Not ugly. Beautiful. Stupid peasants."

I coughed out a laugh. That she would call the present-day Bretons peasants was kind of funny.

"He's dead, the *Bugul noz*?" I asked.

"Not dead, gone. Like us. We just turn to this," she said and held forth the wing, "when we go."

While we admired it, the wing just disintegrated, like a sculpture made of snowflakes being blown away in a fierce winter wind. Nothing remained. Korri Ann grasped after it, but there was nothing left to hold onto. Even though Korri Ann said the wing didn't belong to the *Bugul noz*, it still seemed kind of sad. But where had she gotten it from?

The memory I'd had a glimpse of earlier sprung forth in fullness. Our Korrigan in the Schattenreich had a mound-hut dwelling, covered with moss. Out front was a deep small pool, of cenote deepness. I'd always wondered who got sacrificed there in times past. But I didn't *really* want to know. Inside the hut, well, yes, it had a hobbit-like quality, especially if hobbits were much more sinister creatures than Tolkien had visualized them. And if they could shapeshift. Then they would be Korrigans.

But the important part of the memory was out back of Korri's house. There existed a place I only glimpsed through an oval window and had been admonished to never ever never under any circumstances try to go to. The dying, nearly dead orchard of trees resembled live oak with immense amounts of what I'd always assumed was Spanish moss or stringy spiderwebs hanging from their branches. Very beautifully patterned diaphanous material, like the wing Korri Ann had held in her small hand.

Fenris again raised one of his lush but elegant eyebrows and we exchanged a look.

"You turn into creatures made of that stuff?" I asked and rubbed the bridge of my nose again. It was late, and I sensed I was going to need a lot more Gaelic coffee to get through this.

"That is only a part of us. The rest is invisible. Until we get hungry. Then we're not invisible."

"Hungry," I said and knew instantly where this was going. "For human blood?"

She gave me the Korrigan version of a shrug, very subtle. But the frown on her face told me volumes.

"You turn into non-dead kind of vampire things? Like invisible dragons...or what?"

Her look didn't change. And she didn't look away. "Dragon-like. We...they...don't get hungry very often. Not unless something wanders by. Used to be things could get in from here." She gestured around us, meaning the waking world. "The *Bugul noz* was the one who kept humans safe from wandering in, so they wouldn't get eaten. He made the paths and also scared the mortals away. But since the veil closed, that didn't happen very much anymore." She sat straighter and closed her hands into tight fists. "Now, though, with the veil open…"

"He had too much work to do," I said.

"Too many paths to make. And it used him up."

I sat back and took another sip, letting the coffee, cream, and smoky whiskey flavors blend before swallowing. The fire in my belly made me feel as if things were going to be okay. I knew it was an illusion. As long as the veil stayed open, these kinds of things would keep happening. And ultimately, the fate of the *Bugul noz* was then, without a doubt, our fault.

I sighed.

I wondered how extensive Korri Ann's knowledge of my far-flung family was, some of whom, like Fenris, were not entirely human. Like my other cousin Jörmundgandr, whose name was a mouthful, even for a native-born German. And she was a handful. She's not properly a dragon. I'd guess you could name her serpent. Or wyrm. And an *eigi einhamr*, a

Germanic skinwalker, like Fenris; they were both from the *Jötnar* side of the family. Jörmundgandr's spirit form, which was a dominant part of her personality, was of the Grendel variety. Only not ugly. Orrie, as her siblings called her (much easier to say), was beautiful. And sinister. And she had no wings.

"Dragon-like. You mean the *Bugul noz* is now a big—"

"Is also a Guardian."

"Guardian. Okay. You said that already. Then—"

"You Make things. Can you Make him again?"

"But...the wing is gone. How..." I rubbed my forehead to force my brain to focus. "I don't understand how this can work."

She lowered her head, another tear escaping. The Korri who lived in the Schattenreich was also emotional from time to time. Sad, somehow.

"Is he a Korrigan?" Fenris asked.

Korri Ann opened her mouth to answer, but hesitated. "It's possible. We don't know, just that he's always been there. As we are. But there is only one of him."

"But what does he guard?" I asked.

"He used to guard the sacred place. And the paths."

"Paths…as in the path you took to get through the veil?"

She nodded and two tears slid down her cheeks. "Korrigan paths. Special. For me…us. Paths for the ones left. He makes with his words."

While I thought, I hummed a tune that sounded a little like the gene sequencer in action.

"Wait," Fenris said and held up a hand. "Where is this *sacred* place?"

"Everywhere and nowhere, like all the places in Ande-dubnos," she said.

I leaned forward, my arms across my thighs. One of the big square candles on the table began to sputter. Then another one.

"This is all academic. And I do mean that." I looked up, directing Fenris a critical once-over. "One. How are we supposed to get the *Bugul noz* out of the sacred place in order to remake him?"

Korri Ann sighed and her whole body shook. I waited, but she continued to stare at the candles as if hypnotized.

"Two. If we get him out, I'm still not sure how you think we can restore him."

"Make him," she insisted. "You have done it. I heard of the things you make."

"Have heard of what—"

Right then, a fluffy black bunny hopped in front of Fenris's feet. We all stared at it. Its cashmere fur looked as soft as Fenris's sweater. More crushably soft than the plushiest plush toy.

It lifted its little bunny nose to sniff at us, both ears tilted forward. Fenris leaned over and scooped up the bunny with one hand and put it on his lap.

"How is Ickles?" I asked.

He smiled. Korri Ann pointed to Ickles the bunny. "It is made. You made him."

It was true. Fenris's bunny was one of my more successful designs.

I executed my designs on my own specialized hybrid computer (also assembled by Cousin Jeremiah) and in my favorite color, dark blue, and with a retro keyboard (where the keys clacked), but the programs I ran did not conform to the 2025 Geneva Convention Genetics and Reproduction Protocols. Not by a long shot.

However. The Geneva Protocols only covered reproduction of waking world life. The real world. The kind of genetic designs I worked on in my spare time, my professional hobby, were not the kinds of things you would find in the real world. Their essence was designed to work in the Otherworld. Ande-dubnos. Through our ancient bloodline, we had access to the Otherworld. And we could do things there that most people would call magic.

We called it Schattenwerk. Shadowcraft. All of us of the blood had our specialties. Designing unusual, (magical) shadowcraft creatures was mine. It required manifesting my craft into the waking world, because I hadn't yet been able to construct a fully operating genetic laboratory in Ande-dubnos. Not yet. I had started though. I had started to set up a lab in our Otherworld castle, the equivalent to Burg Lahn, called *Lahn dunum*. I just hadn't had enough time lately to mess with it.

So I interpreted my designs as not *exactly* contravening the Geneva Protocols. What they *exactly* did was sometimes unpredictable. But interesting.

Much more interesting than my doctorate work.

"Korri Ann," I said and cleared my throat.

"Korri Ann?" Fenris said and made a canine-like snort.

I ignored him. "Ickles the bunny is a waking world construct. His…material comes mostly from the same stuff that makes up all life on our planet."

"It is all connected. We are reflections of you," she said, and opened her arms. "We are a part of your Dreams, your memories, your past. Maybe, your future…but that is not known."

I jumped up and walked to the window. It was a problem that now, I knew, would never let me go until I figured it out. Were the Ande-dubnos creatures alive? The Korrigan had just answered the question. They lived. Through us. They were our reflections, as a fun house mirror that shaped and distorted, in this case by time and place and the growth of rationality and modern religions antagonistic to their existence.

The question remained: would it be possible, was it even imaginable, to *remake* Ande-dubnos creatures? Here would have been an ideal opportunity to test out my secret *Lahn dunum* evil scientist laboratory and its capabilities. An opportunity and a danger. Aside from the danger of being eaten by

Korrigan zombie vampires. What kind of new monsters could I make? A funny tickling in my belly made me think that my parents would definitely not be amused by the idea. Or the actuality.

I turned around. Korri Ann now sat on the couch next to Fenris. She stroked Ickles' head.

"Let's go get the *Bugul noz*. Petting bunnies will have to wait until later."

"But how do we get there?" Fenris asked.

"I know how. And it's not far at all. We just have to take a stroll through the Schattenreich."

❀❀❀

I'd crossed with Fenris before to the Schattenreich. It had involved a passionate kiss and a betrayal. This time my family would not be waiting to ambush Fenris after we crossed. I counted that as a positive development in our relationship.

Fenris couldn't yet cross to the Schattenreich on his own. We hadn't given him permission. He had access to a small closed off portion of the Schattenreich that had been formed by his human father, my uncle Kilhian. Deceased.

This time the kiss was just as passionate, but tempered with the experience of learned trust between us.

As with most things having to do with the veil, the less you tried to think about it directly, the easier it became. The kiss deepened and made it hard for me to concentrate on crossing.

The crossing happened effortlessly.

The illusion of dropping, not falling, not exactly, while my body slipped sideways, caused us to break off the kiss. Did crossing the veil feel the same way to him? We opened our eyes at the same time. Fenris smiled. Caught. A wimpy gasp escaped me. Korri Ann had traveled with us by hanging her arms around my neck and making fake gagging noises during our kiss.

"We're here."

"Should we transform?"

"Not yet. I may have to do Schattenwerk and that requires an opposable thumb. And have to hope that it works," I said, mumbling the last part.

We also brought Ickles. It made me sad to do so, but I had to insist over Fenris's objections. I wanted to snicker at his attachment to the bunny. But I didn't. One didn't snicker at lovers. We weren't quite there yet. Maybe wouldn't ever be. So, carefully not snickering.

The meadow clearing with the mostly silent River of Life to my left and the Schattenreich forest to my right was also still in the grip of winter. The grasses felt stiff and dry. The meadow flowers dead until spring. The branches of the deciduous trees – oak, maple, birch, willow – hung leafless and forlorn. A few clothed black pines, reminiscent of a warmer northern European climate, huddled in between.

I gave Fenris's hand a quick squeeze and let go. We headed through the forest. I kept a brisk pace for about half an hour. Korri Ann rode me piggyback while Fenris mumbled, a step or three behind.

I did hear him say clearly at one point, "We'd go faster if we were in wolf form."

I had some sympathy for his annoyance. Fenris was *eigi einhamr*; he had more than one skin. He was a rarity: a Germanic skinwalker inhabiting a twenty-first century male body, the essence of his non-humanity. The pressure to change into his monstrous beautiful wolf form when he was here in Ande-dubnos, even when just in our small neighborhood of it, must have been immense.

When we reached the mound-hut of our Schattenreich Korrigan (just plain Korri), the first thing I noticed was the devastation. Trees had been uprooted and thrown into the cenote in front of Korri's hut, warped sticks dunked in a dark dip of murky water. The vivid green moss that decorated the hut now looked brown and dead. The kludged-together collection of boards that constituted the door lay in pieces in front of the hut. Within was dark and deserted, although I remember it always looking dark and deserted the times I'd been here before.

We halted a few meters away from the hut. I tried to dislodge Korri Ann's arms from my neck, but she wouldn't budge and began to whimper.

"Does it always look like this?" Fenris asked.

I shook my head, a lump in my throat forming when I thought of something bad happening to Korri. "No." My voice came out as a squeak.

Fenris didn't need any more encouragement. He transformed in an instant, the handsome man replaced by a mega wolf. His black fur, shot through with bits of gray and brown and iridescent silver, bristled. His tail stood straight out behind him, a warning for anyone who could read it. With eyes intently focused, coffee-with-cream colored irises almost hidden by the enlarged pupils, he surveyed the ruins.

I entered the hut, the long dark hallway that appeared to slope down, my hands brushing along the smoothly worn, pebble-textured walls.

After a few twists and turns, the hallway opened out into a narrow room lined on one side with crude shelves that looked like shaved pieces of bark with a thin layer of wood still attached. Odd collections of stones, dried leaves and other scavenged debris lined the shelves. On one edge were three chipped teacups in their saucers and a teapot, the spout partially cracked.

Fenris padded up behind me. I set Korri Ann on the tree-trunk table. She let go of my neck reluctantly. The room had a Korrigan-sized wooden door that led to Korri's kitchen, which she never allowed guests to enter. The visual focus of the room was the oval picture window, minus the glass, that dominated the wall just off to the side of the kitchen entrance.

Fenris took a few steps towards the window. There never had been any glass in the window that I could remember, but it looked as if something had come through in a hurry; the window frame and sill were cracked and battered.

I went to stand next to him, my arm across his canine shoulders. Standing, his torso came up to my waist. That's how big he was.

"That's it out there," I said.

He turned his head to spare me a look, but then returned his attention to what was outside the window. The murky twilit grove of sickly trees, their branches being strangled by clumps of a kind of fairy moss, but this moss had never been seen in the waking world. It all formed an eerie landscape unrelieved by birdsong, the scent of rich loam. It lacked strong color, somewhat resembling a sepia landscape with dark shadows lurking everywhere. Not an inviting place to go for an afternoon stroll. I never had, and neither had any of my sibs. We'd been warned against doing any such thing. Many times. Not known for our obedience, in this case we had all complied even if we didn't know what was out there. Even Korri had never suggested we *go take a look*. My father would have incinerated her with one of his Schattenwerk fireballs on the spot.

"What is that stuff?" Fenris growled, the wolf in his voice vibrating through my arm, still draped over him.

"That stuff is what I'm guessing Korri Ann was talking about – the remains of the Korrigans. Their wings."

We both turned to look at the Korrigan. She stared out the window, her eyes bright with a manic gleam, as if she was hypnotized by the spectral tableau. The mossy substance on the trees did not – or did not any longer – bear any resemblance to the delicate wing that Korri Ann had showed me. What remained were now just the tattered remains of wings. Whatever had caused their destruction, the wing-like substance had become something less beautiful, like insect wings, crushed and discarded.

"What happened?" I asked.

"Drained," Korri Ann mumbled, still in her trance.

"By what?"

"*Bugul noz*. Hungry. Angry."

"What keeps them in there?" Fenris asked.

"You mean *kept*," I said. "I'm guessing it was *our* Korrigan, the one who lives – or lived – here in the hut. But what happened to her? And what is the reason for this destruction?"

"He's gone," Korri Ann said in a distressed whisper. Her whole body shook.

"Who's gone? You mean the *Bugul noz*?"

"Some of your people will die," Korri Ann said. "We were afraid of that. That's why I asked you to Make him again. So this wouldn't happen. Should have hurried."

"But what happened to our Korri?" I asked to no one in particular.

"She tried to help him," Korri Ann's timid voice disappeared, replaced by a voice that sounded like something I was familiar with when dealing with Ande-dubnos entities. It sounded like *troidell*...the Breton word for a contrivance or, more bluntly, a trick. "We decided to bring him to you...so you could Make him there in the place where you do the Craft." She took a deep breath and spurted out, "And then he...he must have gotten out." Her lips clamped shut.

"What? Korri...I mean, you and our Schattenreich Korri, planned to bring the *Bugul noz* – or what was left of him – to me in my lab in Cologne...and you are just *now* telling me this?"

"I didn't know she had failed...until we got here." She stuck her nose up in the air.

My skin felt inflamed with anger and I smelled tar and burnt matches. My nostrils flared. I clenched my fists, wanting to hit something. Anything. Korri Ann would do for a start. I could slap her from here to next week. Fenris growled loud and long. Oh, how I sometimes hated Ande-dubnos and all its natural – or unnatural – inhabitants.

"So what is he now doing and where?" I asked.

"He's doing what he always does," she said.

"He's…making paths?" I asked.

She nodded.

"Paths to…in here?" I pointed at the dreadful tree grove.

She nodded again.

The trees outside the window made a nasty creaking sound, like bones clattering.

"You can change back now, Fen," I said. "We have to look elsewhere. And fast."

It seemed the formerly harmless-to-humans Night Shepherd had become a not-so-harmless Night Shepherd in service to Korrigan vampires. Except the ones that had gotten in his way seemed to be have been *drained*. But I guessed there were more that had fled from his wrath and now waited for his return. And the humans who would follow him to their doom.

The question was where to find him.

And Make him again.

Or kill whatever he had become so that it *couldn't* come back.

Part II

Something Found

WE WATCHED THE *Tanzbrunnen* from a short distance away. The 'dancing fountain' was an impressive circular water feature built nearly a hundred years earlier just a stone's throw from the Rhine river. In the middle of the fountain was a raised round open stage roofed with a wavy stretched white sailcloth. I'd been here once for one of my uncle's concerts. His rock-folk-veering-into-folk-metal music, his loyal fans, and the fine atmosphere had made it a magical summer's eve.

We crouched behind some permanent freestanding constructions shaped like convex umbrellas (also with sailcloths) that served as both sunshades and rainshades for visitors. The waters of the fountain were drained for the winter, the place deserted. The *Rheinpark* was deader than dead, the gardens waiting for spring and a horde of gardeners to make them come alive again.

We parked Fenris's sleek Audi sedan – minus chauffeur – in the official parking lot with no one here to question our invasion. One phone call from Fenris got us access to the now deserted lot. I wondered exactly what kind of influence he had here in the city. My mother had told me recently that his father, her evil twin, had had plenty of mojo in Cologne to spend from all his financial connections. He'd been richer than our family and not afraid to throw his influence around to get what he wanted.

Korri Ann thought that a fountain was the most likely place for the *Bugul noz* to make an entryway for his paths. The Korrigans needed to be near water. They weren't water sprites or fairies (don't ever call any of the Folk fairies), but water was an essential part of their existence. She didn't say why. I was tired and hyped up with worry, but I had to know. Korri Ann thought that our Korri *might* have led the *Bugul noz* to water, hoping we'd be able to find her.

Why or how she knew that…I had only nodded.

And wonder what else she hadn't told me.

Water was a tricky proposition in Cologne with its many fountains, not to mention the

Rhine itself. Some 'water features' were classified as wells and some were even old examples of animal troughs. Some dated back to Roman times. We'd already checked the *Heinzelmännchen* fountain in the city center across from the rowdy *Früh Kneipe*, the *Petrus* fountain, and the *Dom* fountain (with its curious mosaic that looks like swastikas, but isn't because it was built around fifty years before the Nazis started fouling the air by taking breaths).

The fountains were all pretty close together, around the Cologne cathedral and the Roncalliplatz, and therefore quick-and-easy to check. No giant evil ugly monster dude with spider silk wings was anywhere around.

Fenris was the one who suggested the *Tanzbrunnen*. It was in the middle of a huge public area that included a beach club direct on the Rhine, the beautiful *Rheinpark* gardens, two theaters in addition to the *Tanzbrunnen* stage for shows, and an outdoor bar/restaurant that was a nice place to sit and have a drink on a summer's evening. I could easily imagine coming back with Fenris for just such an occasion.

Someday.

If we survived this without getting eaten. I wasn't feeling too optimistic.

Especially if the *Bugul noz* was now in Cologne. And if our Korri, with the escaped *Bugul noz* in pursuit, had been forced to choose a place near water to make a path to lead large numbers of humans to be slaughtered by fairy vampires, this was the place to do it.

Fenris half-dozed next to me while leaning against the pillar. Korri Ann fidgeted inside my backpack, her head sticking out and one hand resting on my shoulder. Ickles the cashmere bunny stuck his nose out next to her. His whiskers twitched against my neck.

The alcohol from the Gaelic coffee had worn off, but the caffeine had kicked in, and I felt antsy and uncomfortable in my skin. The air smelled cold and fresh and menacing. I couldn't smell myself under the coat, but I imagined it wasn't pleasant. Not much I could do about that now. Maybe my body (mal)odor would be strong enough to vanquish the *Bugul noz* or knock him out. Not feeling too optimistic about that either.

I snorted, my exhalation making a little cold cloud. Fenris opened an eye, his eyebrow raised.

I shook my head.

In front of us, something shimmery moved. The fountain, which normally took over a day to fill, was full. Spontaneously. It sprang into fountaining, with all the jets on in all their glory and lighted. These weren't the installed lights, which were magical enough, but some sort of otherworldly lights – true fairy lights that appeared to float on top of the water – white and pure and ghostly with a haze of curling, spreading fog and the inviting soft music of bells. I didn't recognize the melody, but it made me start forward.

I was quickly lost in the fog. I could no longer see the fountain or its surrounds. I walked on.

Fenris called my name faintly from somewhere over to my right. I turned in that direction, but the sound ceased.

He called from my left. I turned that way.

Nothing.

The entrancing bells and a sweet fresh scent, like a flower shop heady with carnation and lavender and the sweet delicate powdery fragrance of violets came from ahead of me. I followed my nose.

The fog cleared. I walked on through an alleyway, the backdrop a green-tinged horizon lined with trees with exquisitely textured white bark, only a few of which still grasped their colorful leaves, drained of the green, photosynthesis on hold until spring, the ground strewn with shed leaves in bright fall colors.

I looked down.

I wore white satin slippers and a Regency era sleeveless white ball gown, the skirt trimmed in lace and satin, the bodice in satin and bedecked with tiny pearls. My dark chestnut hair hung long and wavy down my back. My skin seemed paler than usual and had a weird translucent glow that only increased the farther in I went.

Ahead of me was *something* tall and large. He would dwarf even Fenris, with broad heavy shoulders, long legs and arms, and dark hair with streaks of green in loose plaits trailing down his back. He wore a velvet coat and old-fashioned yellow breeches that were stretched across massive thighs, but looked soft and supple and made from animal skin. Two delicate wings extended from his shoulders. Butterfly wings made for a giant, gray and translucent and beautiful, they consisted of a soft and intricate pattern of whorls.

Those wings were the only thing that differed. But the rest was my Beauty and the Beast Dream made real.

I was no Beauty. The other von der Lahn women, my mother and sister, were better candidates for that role. And this Beast walking away from me was not the one I dreamed about. My Beast was a man who hid his wolfskin from the waking world. *My* gray wolf was my spirit animal that I could transform into in Ande-dubnos, but it was a part of me, just as his wolf skin was a part of him. It neither detracted nor added to my basic humanity, but I liked to think it made *me* more *me*, was part of my inner natural self. Was that any different from a Germanic skinwalker?

Very.

Fenris wore his wolfskin without shame and had no wish to be rid of it, to be fully human. Fenris's wolf was big and dangerous to those who opposed him. I had tamed him once, through guile, but it was to save him from being hurt even worse.

In the process, a spark had ignited between us. The spark was there before, when I first laid eyes on him, not knowing who or what he was. He had known who I was, and it was perhaps his recognition and a measure of surprise that had started the whole thing between us.

Do you believe in love at first sight? Me, neither. But I do believe that something happens sometimes, like a finger snap, when two people meet. And that's what happened. Between Fenris and me.

I didn't believe there was a real chance for us to be together. For it to work. My waking world self just didn't believe it. But the Dream, of us, the one that woke me, alone in my bed at night, feverish warm and yearning; that was different. In that dream I was dressed like this, and he was dressed like that. Transported into an era that a slew of romance novels were made of, we danced in his snow-laden garden and the world was ours alone.

We ran together then in that Dream, through the night, through the trees, transformed, two wolves in the grip of the now the speed the movement. Aware of the night and the silence that caressed us.

Transform, came the command. It was a powerful urge, to become my wolf, to run, to catch up with the Beast in front of me, the one who had found and stolen my Dream.

Juliette, came the call from somewhere else, from the voice of my Dream. From Fenris.

Mind awake at Fenris's call, I shook off the Dream and with it the lethargy that had gripped me in the fog that led me here.

I resisted.

Because I knew that if I gave in and went to the thing in front of me, I would die.

No distinct smells, just deadness, and that's how I knew I was in Ande-dubnos. But where? And what was in front of me?

He stopped and turned to face me. *Come to me. This is* your *path.* Before I looked away, I had a glimpse of dark round eyes and a lined face, skin pitted with holes and bumps, and cruel fleshy lips open to reveal many, many uneven teeth. A thick neck and bulging chest.

He was visible. And that meant he was hungry.

He was not ugly. He was worse.

I turned and ran, exchanging the ball gown with the flick of a hand for a simple cotton T-shirt and stretchy leggings, feet bare. Gaining speed. I pushed at hard cold ground that burned the soles of my feet, crunching leaves, trying to chew up distance and just get away.

A tearing, ripping-of-flesh noise from behind caused me to stumble and shudder and want to scream. A snarling growl, as of a large, very large wolf made me spin around fast.

Fenris-as-wolf was grappling with the Regency-clad monster man.

The creature recited something in a short snatch of a deep sing-songy voice, and grabbed onto Fenris, throwing its arms around him.

Fenris appeared dazed for a few moments; his eyes had a druggy look to them. But he shook his head and pushed off the *Bugul noz* – the nattily clad horror could only be him or what was left of him – with his slender but powerful hind legs while snapping at him, massive wolf jaws threatening serious damage.

There was no doubt that Fenris could carry through with ripping the *Bugul noz's* throat out.

They stared at each other for a few seconds. Stalemate.

I took a few steps forward, and reached around to my backpack to grab Ickles. I would have to destroy the bunny to get to the genetically engineered organic polymer inside him. Ickles was one of my best tricks, a piece of Ande-dubnos shadowcraft and *that* had been my real present to Fenris. The polymer could be used to capture the *Bugul noz*. I silently begged Fenris's forgiveness.

But my backpack was not there. I had lost it and the creatures inside it somewhere in the fog.

The *Bugul noz* disappeared. Fenris leapt after him – into nowhere – they were both just disappeared. There followed a loud click-BAM. As of a door. Slamming.

The path was closed.

My knees tensed and my body was ready to bolt again. But there was no one there, no alleyway of trees, no green glow, just rough paving stones and the dead of night.

The thousands of gallons of water that had so recently filled the *Tanzbrunnen* now shimmered, the liquid as ghostly as the fog that had swept me away just a few minutes…hours…ago. Its many jets were quiescent. The fairy lights extinguished. Dawn couldn't be far away. We'd left Fenris's place sometime after midnight, close to 2:00 in the a.m. It was now close to 4:00.

I ran up to where they had stood and fought, Fenris and the *Bugul noz*, and there it was on the ground. The beautiful wing that had been attached to the creature. I stifled a cry. I had no idea where to find them in that ghostly awful sacred place where dead Korrigans went to spend eternity.

And where the fuckall was Korri Ann? Note to my smarter self: never trust a Korrigan ever again.

I picked up the *Bugul noz* wing and felt childlike arms around my neck.

"Korri Ann?"

She hugged me tighter.

"Where is the wolf-man?" she asked.

"He's..." I choked.

I pulled on one arm to bring her around to my side and then grabbed her upper body, holding her in front of me, her mossy dress clasped in one fist, the *Bugul noz* wing in the other. She felt so light, almost as light as the filmy wing, as if she wasn't really made of solid substance at all.

"Where is Ickles?" I asked.

She gulped and pointed to my backpack that lay in a little crumpled pile near the fountain. "He's not damaged, just a little blood. We had to fight off a few of the...others—"

"What others?"

"From my kind, the others that have passed on." She put her arm across her eyes and stifled a sob. Then she ran over and got the pack, tucked Ickles under her arm and dance-hopped back to me. Ickles looked terrified –

frozen in shock, its big bunny eyes glazed over. It had expected to die. It still might. At my hand.

I shook the Korrigan in front of me, not meaning to, but my energy was fast giving out. The adrenaline the fight had produced started to wane. It made me feel sick to my stomach and even more antsy than before. "And Korri?"

She glared at me with a childlike grimace of horror.

"She's gone," I said, a wave of sadness making me dizzy.

"Too late. Not fast enough," Korri Ann said.

In my world, the waking world, Korri Ann, had she been human, would have no doubt been labeled a snowflake. Even for her kind, she gave off that specialness vibe in a way that I'd never noticed in Korri from the Schattenreich. I wondered, again, if it was real.

"Korri Ann," I said, and let her go, taking Ickles the bunny away from her, tucking our only chance of detaining the *Bugul noz* under my arm.

She whimpered and turned her wide-eyed worried glance on me.

"Let's stop all this. I want to you tell me what is really wrong. Right now. Or I won't help you anymore. *Our* Korrigan has *died* because of this."

"Really wrong?" Her accent was detectably British, something I hadn't noticed before.

"Do you want me to *Make* the *Bugul noz*? Is that what we are doing here?"

She opened her mouth. Closed it.

I pointed a finger at her. "Don't lie to me. I'm not threatening you. But I need to know. *Now*."

She sighed, and then it was as if she deflated, the air went out of her and she shrunk even more. "I am not true Korrigan."

"Not...what are you?"

She sank to the ground and put her head in her hands. "Like wolf-man. I was *Jötnar*. Long time now. They put me out. Sent me away. Too small, too ugly to be *Jötnar*. They were...are proud Folk. But stupid, too."

"You are one of Fenris's...I mean of his mother's tribe?"

She shook her head. "No...I mean, maybe. So long ago. I was just a baby. They left me so the Korrigan would take me."

Too tired to stand any longer, I sunk to the ground next to her. My head swam and my arms tingled with the cold, but I hardly felt anything except a stunned sort of exhaustion that made my feet feel like they were encased in lead boots.

"And so you grew up to be a Korrigan."

"Had no choice."

"My father, a very smart man, says, '*Choice is. Always.*'"

She shrugged. "Was okay to be Korrigan."

"But?"

"*Bugul noz*...he does have a name. Long name. Beautiful. He is beautiful. I..." She hugged herself tight.

"You fell in love with him?" A snort escaped me. I couldn't picture the Regency monster dude and the little Korrigan in front of me as a pair.

"Both ways. Love. It was both ways. He was not monster then."

"Mutual. He loved you back."

She sniffled.

"And? What happened?"

"It's not allowed. And I am not Korrigan. He...we thought we could make another one. Of him."

I slapped a hand to my head. "A baby? Is that what this is all about? I don't believe it."

"They kicked me out. Banned. Just like the *Jötnar* sent me away. Broke his heart, it did. He never had a...friend before."

I petted the bunny, maybe a little too vigorously. It stiffened even more. "Let me guess, then. So he kept making his paths for you to get back to…," I paused to make a spirally motion around her, "being able to meet with him. They killed him for it?"

She shifted and put her hands under her tiny thin thighs. I wished I had thighs like that. Sort of.

"Nonono…no not like that. It was as I said. He kept making too many paths. They kept erasing them, to keep me out. It exhausted him. And his heart broke. And he just passed on." Now she broke out in sobs.

I'd never seen any of them so emotional. But she wasn't one of them. She was related to Fenris!

"So this isn't our fault at all. It's not about the veil being torn open. About those who guard the ways. *That* was a lie." I'd finally caught her.

"I didn't say it. You *thought* it."

"I…you implied it."

Somehow my legs propelled me upward, despite the achy feeling. Fenris was still in danger and it was all so not worth it after all. "I'm going to get Fenris. You…you will take me to the path, where they are." I eased the *Bugul noz* wing into my backpack. Carefully.

"Will you still Make him?" she asked, jutting her chin out in defiance.

"Is this a hostage situation?" I asked.

"Hostage?" She looked away.

"Is Fenris a prisoner?"

"Not a very good one, I don't think."

I grabbed her and held more tightly onto Ickles, who tried to squirm out of my grip. I marched over to the fountain, preparing to cross. "Take me," I said, intending to walk right in. "Now."

The Korrigan squealed. And then she took me and Ickles through. The door opened, the fountain gone, we were back in the alleyway of trees. I was not in the Regency dress, but had returned to my battledress of T-shirt and leggings. Since I was last here, what seemed like about ten seconds ago, the trees had lost all their leaves, and were just bare skeletons. The dead leaves were either gray or brown. In the middle of winter-dead, then. Gray iron sky. What *was* the time differential?

Not knowing where to look, I loosened my grip on the Korrigan. She slipped out of my grasp, made herself very small, and started running.

"Not so easy, Miss I'm-not-a-Korrigan."

I waved a hand and threw one of my location spells at her. It would help me track. It used scent and markings, both better than DNA in Ande-dubnos where genetic markers were but a memory, history, of a time long past.

Tracking the Korrigan led me to Fenris. He lay on his side, blood starting to cake on his flank. I rushed to him. He wasn't entirely awake, but lifted his head and nuzzled me with his nose, bruised and also bloodied. I cradled his wolf's head in my arms. He relaxed and breathed out heavily, his eyes closing.

Now that I had Fenris, the problem was to get him back home; wolf or man I didn't care. But in either form, he was too big for me to transport. I didn't know whether the place we were in was a regular part of Ande-dubnos or someplace else, like the Between Lands or even further out. But transporting directly from Ande-dubnos to the waking world was not one of my talents. I could do it easily from the Schattenreich. But here, I'd need an intermediary, or a path.

Just then the *Bugul noz* lumbered into my range of vision. He stood a distance away from me and his body, as such, heaved with the effort of breathing. I'd wonder about that later. He stumbled closer, one step at a time.

I took Ickles by the scruff of his neck, kissed him on the head and wrung his neck, killing him instantly. I died a little inside at that, but I'd mourn him later. His pelt peeled away at his death, and I reached into the mass of his still-warm organs – the stink of a tiny life rudely ended wrinkled my nose – to remove the organic polymer bind.

I waited. The *Bugul noz* came closer. Just a couple more steps. I saw the tiny Korrigan scooting in front of him, waving her arms. He looked down at her, but lurched forward again. She jumped out of his way.

One more step.

He took it. I flung the bind at him and murmured my own chant.

The polymer expanded to accommodate his girth and height. He was wrapped in my *Schattenwerk* construction, Ickles' sacrifice. He was trussed, as my mother would say in her remnant Texas accent, and not going anywhere.

Korri Ann started screaming at me in her tiny tinny voice.

"Help me get Fenris back to the waking world or your *Bugul noz* will stay that way forever," I said, gasping with the strain of holding Fenris. I didn't know if what I told her was true – how long Ickles' polymer would hold – but she didn't need to know that.

Fenris breathed shallowly, his chest rising and falling too rapidly.

I was afraid.

I put my hand over his rib cage, bunching the soft beautiful mélange of brown, rust and black, the ends tinged with silver. He calmed under my touch. I felt for wounds and found two around his ribcage, deep but with surprisingly little blood. Maybe that was a good thing. I just didn't know.

If I had Jeannie's power, I could just blink us back to Fenris's place. But I didn't.

I stared at Korri Ann. She had that power, or something very much like it.

"Get us back," I said through gritted teeth. "Before it's too late. If Fenris dies—"

My voice caught.

She put fists on hips, at least where hips should be – there wasn't much curvature to her – and sniffed. "Now you say is time to hurry."

"Do it!"

Korri Ann stared into the near distance. A path opened up in front of us, obscuring the trees and everything else faded as if part of an unreal backdrop. She gestured at Fenris and he became tiny, a furry lap wolf. I held him tight in my arms and followed that path as if my life depended on it.

In a way, it did.

Part III

Something Made

TIME TO HEAD to the lab and transform.

Not to my spirit wolf. It was time to embrace my evil mad scientist.

We'd left phones, flimsies, and laptops at Fenris's place since we'd expected to cross the veil. Even if they'd traveled with us, they wouldn't have been any use. I hugged my laptop to my chest. My backpack was on my lap on the drive from Fenris's place to the Uni.

I paid the taxi driver and was hurrying along the sidewalk before he even pulled away from the drive.

Time to Make the *Bugul noz*. And it needed to go down fast.

Once inside the lab, I pushed up the lid. My laptop went live. I pounded keys and sent programs to run.

I checked the QuickWomb™ to make sure there was nothing else brooding in there.

It would soon have something new. I pushed buttons and called on my shadowcraft so that the creature I was about to make registered as something mundane, like mice clones, rather than what was actually gestating in there. In the meantime, the gene sequencer beeped that it had finished analyzing Fenris's blood sample, much quicker than I thought. I extracted a few drops of my own blood after pricking my finger – I already had my DNA on file in my computer.

That there wasn't any genetic material from the *Bugul noz* to work with – any waking world material – was just something I would have to live with. Improvisation in science was a highly underrated activity. I added the essence – as close as I could extract it – from the torn gossamer wing from the *Bugul noz* to the genetic cauldron I was making.

I used one of the denuded bunny stem cells we had on reserve to deposit the material in. They had proved the easiest and most reliable animals to use for my shadowcraft experiments. Maybe because of their affinity for being pulled out of magical hats over the past few centuries...well, humanity's superstition and Ande-dubnos reality were definitely connected. So not so far-fetched. Whether the new improved *Bugul noz* would be downsized on account of that was something I would just have to wait to find out.

Appropriately enough, the QuickWomb resembled a toddler-sized toy oven, but made out of metal instead of wood. I wasn't sure myself what was going to come out of it, certainly not mice, and, with a significant probability, something much, much larger than a regular-sized housecat, the limit to the QuickWomb's capabilities.

But this wasn't an ordinary organic print job. The lab swam with shadowcraft, potential and actual, swirling bright clouds of blue and deep gold reminiscent of a van Goghian starry night. These were eddies of power, invading reality. Visible to me, perhaps an uncomfortable feeling to others. I breathed in the sweetness of fresh mown grass and bay laurel, not unpleasant.

A good sign.

The manifestation of my shadowcraft in the waking world was unique to me. It caused a tightening in my belly, a nausea that quickly passed, but was the sign that I had called forth my craft. It was limited to the act of biological creation, as my sister Jax's shadowcraft was attached to her music and my brother Theo's to his science – the structure of the cosmos.

We'd never discussed with each other the particulars – the how and the why and the what-the-fuck. Some things were best kept secret, even to former wombmates.

Usually, when I did my printing, whatever came out *could* come in handy sometime. It or a variation thereof. I'd had to destroy the results more times than I was comfortable with, but there was no other way to handle a biogenetic experiment gone bad. I'd never attempted to print anything remotely close to being sentient. Until now.

These kinds of experiments were my life's work. The life I'd chosen. I needed the front of my doctorate study in biogenetics to give me the freedom to do the things I wanted to do.

My parents had no idea. They'd object. Strenuously. My three siblings (and my cousin Jeremiah) did know, to a certain extent. They kept my secrets, and I'd keep theirs.

Unless something went terribly wrong.

Which could happen. Like right now.

Good things had happened. Like Ickles the bunny that I'd printed for Fenris. His black fur, soft as a quiet autumn night, his dark blue eyes like my father's. Midnight blue. I'd made Fenris promise not to rend Ickles on one of his wolf hunts. He could buy a pet shop variety rabbit if he wanted to do that. I'd explained to him about the rabbit's gut, a special polymer that could be used to bind a monster.

And it had worked. That I'd had to destroy the little bunny made me sad. But it had been in dire need. I'd once bound Fenris that way.

When I first brought the bunny to him, Fenris thanked me with a gentle kiss and went about constructing a rabbit pen in the small town garden of his immaculate posh flat. When I next saw Fenris, the rabbit was riding around on his shoulder. And he'd house-trained Ickles, he'd informed me.

I told him that one didn't name rare Ande-dubnos protective devices.

He had shrugged and given me one of his posh smiles, a Grantian Smile, somewhere on the scale between Cary Grant and Hugh Grant, and there's not a bad point anywhere on that axis. Yeah, I know. I'm a sucker for old romance movies (and television series). The older the better.

The QuickWomb hummed. Feeling the shadowcraft hum through *me*, like a strong electric current, like acupuncture gone mad, I turned my back on the machine slow and easy. It was pure superstition, the feeling that the machine could implode from too much power. At least I assumed it was superstition.

The clock indicated a slower gestation period than I was comfortable with. I'd have to come back tomorrow afternoon. Doable. Sundays, the lab was even deader than Friday nights. I took deep slow breaths and gathered my things.

Time enough to check if Fenris still lived.

I called a taxi, blinking in the harsh Saturday afternoon sunlight. Fatigue descended.

❀❀❀

I'd laid him on his large, very comfortable-looking bed with a beach-sized towel underneath to catch blood or other leaking fluids. He'd reverted to mega-wolf-sized wolf when we gained the inside of his flat. He lay there still. Immobile, his jaws partly open, a thread of drool visible on the towel. Korri Ann was nowhere to be seen. I didn't much care. She'd have her prize soon enough. I hoped she'd be happy with it because it was all she was going to get from me.

Fenris seemed to be sleeping more easily. Maybe the *Bugul noz* phantom had sent him some good Dreams. Did he dream about me?

The skin around the wounds didn't look swollen. His breathing had deepened even though it was still a little bit ragged.

I wet a washcloth (black cotton terrycloth) in the bathroom sink (smart, black marble countertop, amazing roomy shower stall). After wiping Fenris's fur clean and dribbling on drops of hydrogen peroxide for good measure, I sat in the room's only chair, a roomy and comfortable lounger, determined to stay awake.

When I woke, sunlight was streaming through the blackout shades that weren't entirely drawn, a few rays landing on my face. I turned to look at the patient, and I imagined that Fenris breathed easier. A glance at the bedside clock, another ugly antique, white with gilded gold edges and Roman numerals, told me that I'd slept straight through the late afternoon and evening and it was early Sunday morning. I sighed in relief that there were still a few hours left before the QuickWomb was done.

The gaudy antique clock amidst the upscale, very masculine bedroom, clean and minimal; that was the conundrum of Fenris. Like the furnishings in his apartment, he was a combination of old, ancient old sometimes, but modern in his thinking and his basic humanity. That he hadn't changed back to his man-form when we'd returned to the waking world was a revelation.

None of us, of the blood, had ever to my knowledge manifested our spirit animals in the waking world. But I was a bare twenty-four years old. What did I know of such things? Fenris's skin was a part of him no matter which realm he occupied, so maybe that explained it, though I'd never seen him in his wolf form in the waking world before.

My bicycle was still out front. A quick inspection of the bike lock showed at least one person had tried to tamper with it. I hoped their fingers were still smarting from the shock. I rode it home in the crisp clear air, feeling a chill in my bones that wasn't entirely due to the cold late January air.

Once at my tiny apartment, I picked up dirty pajamas off the floor, shook the duvet into a less crumpled form, and emptied the trash. The forced busywork did nothing to dissipate the uneasiness I'd felt since finding Fenris injured, despite his now being out of life-threatening danger.

I took a shower and changed into my most comfortable flannel-lined jeans. A slouchy loose-knit gray pullover that I'd stolen from my sister Jax went on over a tissue-thin, long-sleeved tee. The clothes were relatively clean, as they had only sat on the floor for a couple of days. I slipped on soft sheepskin boots and wool socks – not cashmere – and then decided to walk back to the Uni for the fresh air and to think, stuffing my laptop and handwritten notes into a cross-shoulder messenger bag. I'd have to walk fast to get there before the gestation was completed. I wasn't sure what to do with the *Bugul noz*, but letting him loose was not a viable option. My nervousness and general feeling of something ominous about to descend on me guaranteed my steps would be quick.

Something lost, something found, something made and something bound.

The words echoed again in my head, and again, it wasn't my inner voice. Someone else was speaking. I still didn't know where the words had come from, but knew I had heard them or read them somewhere before. I tried to remember if they were part of one of my Great Aunt Bertha's trove of fairy tales, but the exact memory eluded me. Was it her voice? It could have been, but I wasn't sure.

The ice skating rink on the south end of the Heumarkt sparkled in the sun. The cobblestones were still slick with morning dew, and the frigid air hurt going into my lungs. I turned right near the trams and headed towards Neumarkt, taking the long way along mostly deserted Sunday morning streets.

The shops were all closed. Only a few bakeries were open, and the doughy smell of freshly baked bread and the enticing fragrance of pastries made my stomach gurgle and then roil. Food would have to wait until this was over.

Something lost was the *Bugul noz*, surely. And we had found him again. Korri Ann had found him, her secret love. Whether he would be the same *Bugul noz* that I returned to her was doubtful. But he, or something very similar to him, was being made. It had a little bit of Fenris and a little bit of me as well. But something bound? I didn't have a clue about that one.

When I got to the lab, the feeling of disaster deepened. I opened the door to find broken glassware strewn about. The stainless steel latches on the QuickWomb had been popped open, not broken but bent. It was empty, although the clock showed another half an hour incubation time.

The new and improved version of the *Bugul noz* had been liberated. Korri Ann. The iron on the QuickWomb latches must have burned her when she'd pried them open. I wonder if she sobbed while doing it. She had decided he was ready and didn't want to wait any more. I jogged up and down the corridors, peering into labs and offices, hoping to find them, a renegade Korrigan and her Night Shepherd. But they were well and truly gone. I held out no hope that the experiment was a success.

Something made. But what?

I'd have to go in search of them.

With heavy sighs and a heavy heart, I spent the next hour and a half cleaning up the lab. I called on my shadowcraft again to repair the QuickWomb; that was my choice, one I might regret. It was a stopgap measure until I could do something more permanent and elegant, but it might just be the push I needed to step up the pace on completing my Otherworld laboratory.

After things looked normal again, it was time to go and look in on Fenris.

Part IV

Something Bound

THE DEEP BREATHS came and went in little puffs of cloud. I'd messed up and *Made* something that I shouldn't have. And now it was on the loose.

Messed up. Big Time. And not only the laboratory. I'd taken the time to clean up the mess, because...covering my tracks was also important. Part of me hoped, intensely, that I could still fix the rest. Help was needed. I had only one option.

It was time to call my father. Something I should have done before things went south (something my mother was fond of saying, although for some reason, her exclamations usually included the back end of a horse). I gestured excitedly while talking to my father on my ancient digital phone instead of just pinging him. This was too complicated for texting. My father listened. And listened some more. He agreed to meet me at my apartment.

I stood before Fenris's door a few minutes later, breathing hard. The key turned in the lock, but the door opened on its own.

Expecting to gaze into Fenris's intense amber eyes, I was surprised to see a complete stranger staring out at me.

"Uh," I said.

"Frau von der Lahn?" he asked me.

I gulped and nodded. He wasn't a complete stranger, I realized, but I'd never seen him when he wasn't behind the wheel of an Audi sedan.

"I was looking for Fenris, for Herr ar C'hoed," I stammered.

"He's not presently here," Fenris's chauffeur said. "He left this for you."

I took the creamy gray envelope from the man. He smiled kindly at me, but not too kindly.

"Thank you," I managed to say, but it felt like someone else speaking. "Did he say…" I shook my head.

"I believe you will find the information you are looking for in his communiqué," he said.

I nodded again, feeling stupid and awkward. I didn't even know the man's name. "I'm sorry, I don't know—"

"Felix Oskar. Just call me Oskar," he said and smiled. The kindness was not feigned, even though he presented a formal front. Maybe the formality was a part of him. That didn't surprise me in the least. He wasn't human, but could pass for one. He was at least half *Tud*. I wondered which lonely corner of Ande-dubnos Fenris had found him in.

"*Auf wiedersehen*," I said and turned to go. He coughed. I turned back.

"If you require my assistance, at any time for any reason, I am at your disposal." He bowed and handed me a business card with a digital imprint that buzzed in my hand.

"I appreciate it," I said.

He closed the door.

I stumbled down Fenris's front steps. And ran.

I slowed a block or so later when I felt a presence, as if someone was following me.

I stopped and turned quickly. The man stopped, too.

"Papa! What are you doing here?"

"Taking a Sunday stroll with my daughter in downtown Cologne," my father said. "Where are we going?" His gentle smile warmed me as he moved to my side. He had on a gray wool overcoat, finely brushed lambswool, and the silly misshaped navy scarf my mother had knitted for him. It had become even more ragged over the years. His dark chestnut hair, nearly the same shade as mine but streaked with silver, hung a little longer than usual, reaching the collar of his coat.

"To my apartment. I thought we were meeting there."

"And how is Fenris?"

"He's not feeling well, and I wanted to look in on him."

My father nodded as if he understood more than I was saying. I had left Fenris out of my explanations to him on the phone. But he had somehow figured out the missing link.

We walked together through Cologne side streets, now busy with pedestrians out for a late lunch or coffee and cake with friends and family. The pubs had also started filling up.

"Want to tell me what else is bothering you?" my father asked.

"You mean besides escaped *Bugul noz* creatures and wayward Korrigans?"

"Besides that, yes. Did something happen between you and Fenris?"

How did he know these things? "I thought only Mama had that kind of intuition," I said.

"Do you want to know the first word you spoke to me?"

I nodded.

"Mama," he said.

I laughed. "I never was very smart as a kid."

"Your mother thought it was brilliant. She'd just...just come back from the Lands Beyond, and I'd been caring for the three of you since your first weeks of life...as a 'single' parent."

"Aha. Then not so stupid?"

"I didn't think so. It was a genuinely blissful moment for me."

I let the silence build as we neared my apartment. He had let me lead.

"How do you know where Fenris lives?"

"Juliette. I am your father."

"That's your answer?"

He laughed. "You mother was here once. She told me, not gently I might add, that I'd find you here."

His confession made me smile. "Papa, did you ever do anything stupid, I mean really unbearably stupid?" I asked.

"You mean, things like trading my youth for power? Or incurring a *geis* from Cathubodua that left me in a coma and nearly cost me everything, including your mother?"

His eyes held a hint of sadness, of regret and chances lost.

"Oh yeah. Those kinds of things."

"Which flavor of stupid do you think you've done? I mean, only if you want to tell me."

I shook my head while I thought, then stuck my hands deep in my pockets. My scarf and gloves were still hanging on Fenris's coat rack, where I'd forgotten them earlier this morning in my haste to leave. The air had not warmed much, but the sun felt good on my face.

"Well, that one time I lost my Siamese cat, Purrface. I've never gotten over that."

My father looked over at me. "That was regrettable, but I wouldn't say it was your fault, except perhaps the *name*. He just decided he wanted to live in the wild rather than curled up in your bed. Purrface, if I recall, wasn't a particularly bright cat."

"No, but he was mine, and I lost him…through neglect. I took him for granted. It was awful. I thought he was dead, locked in one of the cellar rooms or eaten by one of the creatures the Burg uses to protect itself. He *was* a stupid cat, but I loved him."

My father didn't comment, just waited for me to continue.

"That made me afraid to form any attachments with people. That they would leave me, like Purrface."

"Really?" he asked, his tone skeptical.

"Well, yeah, except for Jax, Theo and Brev…and you and Mama and Heiner. And

Opa. And Tante Bertha. Oh, and Gesine. And Jeremiah and Lissy. And Uncle Gus and Aunt Susanna. And Frau Morelos. And…"

My father's crooked smile told me I was being stupid again.

"Okay, I mean the idea of a, you know, love story kind of attachment."

"I didn't want that either at your age. No hurry in your case, really, as far as I am concerned," he said, the hint of irony in his voice exaggerated to make me laugh.

I did laugh. I was a Daddy's girl, more than Jax who worshipped our Uncle Heiner. My father and I had always been close. My parents had avoided having 'favorites' among their four children, but there was a cerebral connection, me with my father. We had a similar way of approaching problems, and that engendered deep affection between us that the others just didn't have.

I sighed and waved my hands around. "I've messed everything up. There's a dangerous creature on the loose that I've created. Fenris is injured. And Korri is dead. And I repaired some lab equipment with *Schattenwerk*…"

"Hmm. I am assuming you will be able to rectify the lab equipment problem?"

I nodded. "It will be okay."

"It is a shame about Korri. She served a useful purpose for a very long time. As for Fenris, well, did he leave you a message?"

"How—"

"He contacted me as well."

"He…what?" I nearly screamed at him.

"Before we talk about Fenris, there's something else."

"The mess I made. And people, they're in danger," I said, trying to keep my voice from turning into a sob.

Hagen von der Lahn, my father, the baron of Burg Lahn, successful philanthropist, and one of the Guardians of the Opening to the veil between the waking world and Ande-dubnos, offered me his arm. He had broken an army of female hearts in his youth, and was still an exceedingly handsome man.

I always felt happy in his presence, secure that I belonged to him, even when he wasn't happy with me. I was puzzled that he didn't display any displeasure at any of the things I'd confessed to him. But I was even more disturbed that Fenris had contacted him.

"I want to show you something," he said and pulled my arm through his.

"Where are we going?" I asked.

"There's a *nemeton* nearby, the location of a former Roman temple that was built on top of an even more ancient spot used by Celts. It's easy to cross there."

"Cross? In broad daylight? Is it far?"

"Not far at all. Just around the corner." My father smiled. "But of course. We only need a few shadows, and the sun's going behind a big raincloud."

❀❀❀

I was a little breathless when we arrived at Korri's hut. Fatigue and stress chipped away what was left of my strength. The front door was now repaired, although no more sophisticated than it had been – a few boards nailed together – and as dilapidated as the old one. The door was closed. The deep pond in front of Korri's house had been cleared of its tree trunks. The water was a clear deep blue-green again, free from debris. The air of desolation was gone.

"Did you call the emergency clean-up squad?" I asked.

He laughed. "Something like that occurred, but it wasn't me." He pulled open the door and gestured inside with a sweep of his arm. "After you."

We made our way into the room that served as a dining/consultation room, the one that afforded a view into the space that contained the dead Korrigans. That was where I had saved Fenris and detained what remained of the *Bugul noz*.

The formerly dented and damaged window frame had also been repaired, and the oval picture window looked out, as usual, onto a perpetual winter landscape of skeletal trees and wings made of spider-silk, the only visible parts of the no-longer extant creatures. I took a few paces towards it and then stopped and turned to face my father.

"What happened?" I asked. "The place was trashed the last time we were here."

"We?" he asked.

"Fenris, one of the Korrigans – I call her Korri Ann – and me. We came in search of the *Bugul noz* or whatever remained of him."

The door to the kitchen squeaked open a crack. I backed up toward my father.

The door opened and Korri Ann stepped through.

She looked almost angelic, not like a mischievous little Korrigan at all. Her face had changed, revealing something I could only classify as happiness.

Anger shot through me, and at the same time pity welled up. I tried to fight the latter. She scooted into the room, her mossy linen dress covered in even more bits of bark and stuck-on leaves than the last time I'd seen her. Her hair, turned a sparkling pure white, flowed in gentle waves around her shoulders. She had on pink ballet slippers. Not wanting to think about where she'd stolen them from, I opened my mouth to speak.

But before any words came out, another creature emerged from the kitchen. He wasn't as big as the monster *Bugul noz* I'd captured earlier, but he did bear a resemblance. He also wore a look of happiness. And Korri Ann was right – he wasn't ugly.

Of course, he did carry some of Fenris and some of me, so he couldn't be all monster.

And it showed. Not a pretty face unless maybe you were a Korrigan. He had the same crazy greenish-dark plaits that stuck out all over his head. And he still had fleshy lips, but they weren't scary gross. Bulky on top, smaller-proportioned on the bottom, he had a kind of a hulk thing going on.

No wings. So I had succeeded. The Night Shepherd had been remade.

I sighed.

We left them a few minutes later, and my father explained some things on our way back to the Schattenreich clearing where we would make our crossing back to Cologne.

"I've offered them sanctuary as long as they fulfill the job that Korri did – keeping the things outside that window from getting into the Schattenreich. They seemed very happy about it all."

"Yeah, I think they're very happy to be together. If the other Korrigans find out, it could cause trouble."

"Not on our turf. The Korrigans can't stage a massive presence in the Schattenreich. It's just not possible."

I nodded. It's what we'd always been told. "But since the veil is open..."

"We've warded the borders solidly over the years and put in protections. There are creatures who are permitted to cross from Ande-dubnos to the waking world, but they don't make detours through the Schattenreich."

I hoped he was right for Korri Ann's sake.

As my father and I sat in the grassy clearing, my eyes misted over thinking about my crossing with Fenris earlier...had it only been yesterday...and our kiss. He wouldn't need that kind of contact with me once we officially gave him the right to cross into the Schattenreich without a chaperone. But that hadn't yet happened. I took out the envelope from Fenris that I'd brought with me. My father sat patiently, waiting. I opened it and read it silently. It was as if Fenris was standing in back of me, the words landing gently on my ear, his voice soft in a way I wasn't used to. His intimate voice that I'd never really heard but so wanted to.

Dearest Juliette,

My apologies for leaving without saying farewell, but you have left me no choice.

Our blood has mingled and, although I expect you didn't know what you were doing, you have put me in an awkward, even difficult situation. Exchanging blood among our people in the Lands Beyond has significance. I'm sorry to say, I have to handle the situation immediately.

Or there could be serious repercussions.

There might be anyway.

So that is why I have to leave.

I don't know when I'll return. At the latest, when the repercussions have settled. At the earliest, well, don't expect me before the trees begin to bud out in Cologne.

In the meantime, you need better protection. Therefore, I entreat you to stay at my flat until I return, where Oskar will be able to look out for you.

Try not to mess the place up too much.

I have already spoken with your father.

Oh, and thank you for saving my life.

Until we meet again,

Yours,

Fenris

I frowned heavily at my father.

"He has informed me that he will be officially courting you when he returns," my father said.

"He what?"

My father shrugged. "It seems the two of you are now bound in some way?"

I nodded. "Our blood. I used it to remake the *Bugul noz*."

"Ah. And mingled blood in the art of creation constitutes some sort of bond, then, among the *Jötnar*."

I shrugged. "He wants me to stay at his place until he comes back. Seems to think I'll need protection."

"Very mysterious. But I'd like you to take him up on it. You can keep your apartment, of course."

"Naturally, especially since you own the whole building."

He smiled. "You found that out, did you?"

"The von der Lahns have never been squeamish about owning real estate," I said in a snobby upper-class German accent.

"With good reason."

I sighed and then remembered. "Something bound!"

"What?"

"Something lost, something found, something made, and something bound. It's a phrase that popped into my head before all this happened." I ticked off on my fingers. "Something lost *and* something found *and* something made was the *Bugul noz*. But something bound – that, apparently is me and Fenris."

"I see. A prophecy." He held out a hand to me. I took it and clasped it tightly. "The von der Lahn women have been known to make them from time to time."

"Papa...I don't know what to do about Fenris. I mean, he's—"

It was my father's turn to tick off items. "He's your cousin. He's not entirely human. And he's dangerous."

"All that." I didn't want to tell my father that I rather liked the dangerous part. But then again, the way he was eyeing me, I didn't have to.

"It will work out. Trust your instincts. And prophecies…well, it seems it has all come true then."

"I'm so sorry for everything, Papa."

He stood, pulling me with him. "You're all grown up. It's time you made some unbearable stupid mistakes. In this case, I think you did rather well."

I wasn't sure what he meant by that, but let it go for now. "If I'd called you to begin with, none of this would have happened."

"Maybe it would have gone down differently, but *something* would have happened."

I closed my eyes in preparation to crossing back. I only hoped we wouldn't scare the daylights out of any wayward pedestrians.

"Juliette…you didn't say whether you were upset at the possibility of being courted by Fenris."

"No, I didn't. Because I have no idea what that means or how I feel about it."

The voice of the man I most looked up to in this world and any others became soft and light, unlike Fenris's. "You have time now to think about it. That's a very good thing."

I needed to make my own path, like the *Bugul noz* made paths to keep humans and Korrigans safe. I had time to do that and to find my way. Unlike Purrface, Fenris had promised to return. I would work on strengthening the path that led to his return, among others of my own making. Thinking about him being gone made my heart ache, but in a good way. A fond way.

I planned on enjoying every minute of it.

I wondered if I would have that Dream of us again when I slept in his apartment. Or maybe now some other ones, definitely not of the fairy tale variety.

About the Author

SHARON KAE REAMER is a speculative fiction writer, American expat, and was a senior scientist the University of Cologne for two decades, teaching and working (mostly) on archeoseismological projects.

In addition to the usual science fiction and fantasy tropes, she loves mysteries and stories that delve into ancient religions and reinterpret them and historical work of all sorts.

She lives in the 'burbs' on the outskirts of Cologne with her family and two tuxedo cats, Loki and Finn MacCool (who are also family but insist on being singled out as feline and referred to by name).

Visit her at https://www.sharonreamer.com

Also by Sharon Kae Reamer